"You Don't Look Like Your Mother," Said the Robin to the Fawn

"You Don't Look Like Your Mother," Said the Robin to the Fawn

by Aileen Fisher

designed and illustrated by Ati Forberg
lettering by Paul Taylor

bowmar

...to Karle

The robin perched
where aspens grow
and peered into
the ferns below.

"Whose child are you
down there," she said,
"with spots of white
on brownish red?"

The fawn looked up
and twitched an ear:
"My mother
is a tan-gray deer."

"A deer!" The robin
sat up tall.
"How does she know
you're hers at all?
With dapples big
and dapples small,
You don't look like your mother"

The robin stared,
her head aslant.
"Whose child is on
that milkweed plant,"
she asked, "with stripes
of white and black
and yellow curved
around his back?"

The caterpillar
blinked an eye.
"You ask," he said,
"whose child am I?
My mother
is a butterfly."

"A butterfly!"
the robin cried.
"You're not like any
I have spied.
You're long and round
not thin and wide.

You don't look like your mother."

Beside the pond,
upon its brink,
the robin bent
her head to drink.

"Whose child are you?"
She cocked an eye
as someone's head
and tail swam by.

"Who, me?"
exclaimed the polliwog.
"My mother
is a hoppy frog."

16

"A hoppy frog?
How can that be?"
the robin cried
excitedly.
"You don't look like
a frog to me.

You don't look like your mother."

"What yellow balls
of fluff are these?"
the robin chirped.
"They float with ease
like little bobbing
puffs of sun
moving softly
one by one."

18

A ball of yellow
wagged its head.
"Our mother
is a duck," it said.

"A duck!" the robin cried.
"All white
and feathered-smooth
and watertight?

20

I really can't
believe it, quite.
You don't look like your mother."

"Whose babies
can these squeakers be
inside the knothole
in this tree?"
the robin asked.
"I cannot think
whose children are
so small and pink."

A squeaky voice
inside the house
said (squeak!),
"Our mother is a mouse." 25

"A mouse all gray
and velvety?"
the robin asked.

"How can it be
she knows you're hers?
It's plain to see
You don't look like your mother."

The robin fixed
a beady eye
upon a stream
that ambled by.
"Whose child, so squat
and strangely built,"
she thought, "goes darting
through the silt?"

"Me?" The insect
gave a slip
of its unusual lower lip.
"If you would like
a straight reply,
my mother
is a dragonfly."

30

"A dragonfly!"
The robin frowned.
"The kind that flies
and darts around
on gauzy wings?
Can it be true?

There's not a sign
of her in you.
You don't look like your mother."

Then to her nest
the robin flew.
She laid five eggs
of greenish blue.

She brooded them
as robins do.

And then
the strangest thing occurred.

Each robin egg
produced a bird.
What naked,
scrawny chicks,
my word!

But did the robin
seek a clue
and want to know,
"Whose chicks are you?"

38

And did she ever
doubt? Oh, no.
She cared for every one
just so,
and sang
"You're wonderful, although

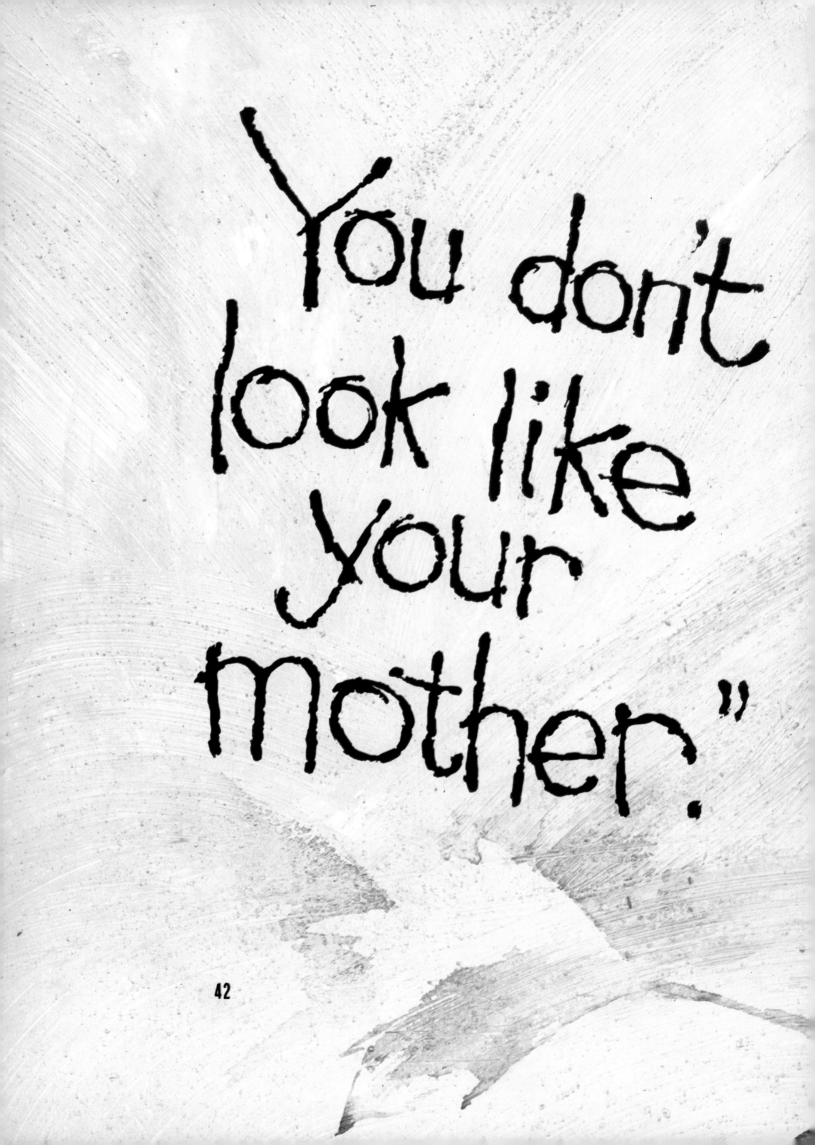

You don't look like your mother."

42